BUBBLE GUM & BANANA-BISCUIT BOY

Book 2:

A NEW RIVAL

THIS BOOK BELONGS TO

....

S&G
Productions

Written By
Seraphina & Gabriel Ciobanu

BLURB:

"Help, it's out of control!!!"
Enter the second book of Bubble Gum Girl and
Banana-Biscuit Boy as they discover a universe far from
their own, a land where no-one has been before,
or have they? This could potentially uncover
a secret that could change their lives forever.

Bubble Gum Girl & Banana-Biscuit Boy

Book 2: A New Rival

Written By: Seraphina & Gabriel Ciobanu

CONTENTS:

She couldn't talk, she couldn't eat, her movements were *sluggish*, only then she realised what had happened...
"*Wake up sleepy head!*" Gabriel yelled.
The siblings had got so tired playing with their new awesome powers, they had fallen asleep (it was hard not to when you've just fought a hoard of demon teachers then relaxed on a SUPERRRRR fluffy cloud).
Gabriel pulled Seraphina to her feet and commented, "You know how people speak about 'bucket loads...' well you dribbled a bucket load in your sleep!" They both peered through the clouds.
"I don't remember that shimmering lake below!" Seraphina said. Gabriel informed her it was her dribble NOT a lake.
Meanwhile, the Supreme Ruler (the children's big BIG boss) thought BIG thoughts. The children loved their new powers but they needed to be used for the greater good as they seemed to be having too much fun with them lately and not using them for a '*higher purpose*.'
"Finally," the Supreme Ruler huffed, "Gabriel and Seraphina.....oh ahem, excuse me, Bubble Gum Girl and Banana-Biscuit Boy, you have a new adventure to attend to, go in search of it."
"Really? I thought we would at least have a week off, maybe take a luxury trip to Hawaii? I mean, can't you just teleport us there with a suitcase full of money? You are the *Supreme Ruler* after all, good at your job, wise, amazing... " Gabriel waffled on hopefully.
"Yes, I AM the Supreme Ruler and flattery won't work; it's your duty not a burden or a paid job," the Supreme Ruler boomed putting the children swiftly back in their place. "Now go, use your powers wisely," he said sternly. Seraphina and Gabriel rolled their eyes, gave a brief wave then pitched

themselves off the cloud.

"This is fun though isn't it!" they agreed.

Just then they landed on a springy, pink bubble and a puff of apple essence seeped out as their feet made contact.

SPROING!!!

"From this point on, we shall be known as Bubble Gum Girl and Banana-Biscuit Boy!" they chorused grinning at each other.

"Hey, do you have any idea where this new adventure is taking place?" questioned Bubble Gum Girl.

"No idea. Hang on, there's school!" Banana-Biscuit Boy cried, pointing in the direction of the red brick building. "Luckily, it's still standing and hasn't been destroyed by weird creatures or random meteorites?!"

Yep, just then, in one foul swoop, as if on cue, a meteorite came blasting out of nowhere and destroyed the school! Immediately, a tonne of white vans pulled up outside and science teachers clambered out dragging their paraphernalia behind them to inspect the random meteorite.

"You and your big mouth!" Bubble Gum Girl reprimanded, glaring at him. Banana-Biscuit Boy swiftly jumped out of the way narrowly avoiding **lasers** that shot at him from his sister's eyes. Any remnants of sleepiness had been erased from Bubble Gum Girl's head and both children had rather blackened faces from the explosion.

"Oh well," Banana-Biscuit Boy said, composing himself. "We can't go back now."

"So what should we do?" Bubble Gum Girl asked.

When they weren't having adventures, school was a major part of their life. With its tattered green sign and empty playground, it had been a familiar place so it was almost sad to see it go and now it had been demolished there would be barely anything to do to occupy themselves.

"Let's try and look for the adventure, although I don't quite know how we'll find it; I guess it will just find us," Banana-Biscuit Boy responded. So they both climbed into Bubble Gum Girl's cloud-skimming *airship* and set off. But instead of going *forwards*, they went **uP**. "Why are we going up?" Banana-Biscuit Boy asked whilst peering through the dense clouds in vain, "I thought you knew how to control this thing?"

"I don't know," his sister answered whilst repetitively leaping on the 'down' lever, frantically trying to change directions.

"So you don't know how to control this thing even though it is your own vehicle?" questioned Banana-Biscuit Boy beginning to wish he had not agreed to her driving. They went higher and higher into the sky and eventually into space.

"HELP," they yelled in unison.

The siblings had never dreamt they would actually fly so high, only astronauts had travelled through this infinite galaxy and the children were pretty sure they were not astronauts.

Just then a monstrous black hole appeared.

"**Wow, didn't see that coming,**" Banana-Biscuit Boy said, dumbfounded.

Bubble Gum Girl started on one of her educational speeches: "Did you know…" her brother groaned, "that this is called a monster black hole as it eats one star per day and it's the closest black hole to earth...oh yeah and by the way we need to go through it."

"**Or that!**" said Banana-Biscuit Boy in a small voice, "But why?"

In one swift ninja like move, she grabbed her brother and yanked him in.

"AGHRRRRRRR!!!" he shrieked, he was totally caught off guard, (you would be too if your, usually sensible sister just pulled you into a monster black hole that eats one star per day and is the closest to earth). No living human being has ever attempted to throw themselves into one, that only happens in comics...right?

SQUELCH!

They landed in a sticky heap. "Where are we?" Banana-Biscuit Boy questioned looking very bewildered.

"Let me explain." His sister looked concerned and anxious whilst scanning her surroundings; she took a deep breath: "This is where Chewing Gum boy lives. I was raised in the other dimension, Bubble Gum dimension and I was born to be rivals with Gum Boy who lives here, look there he is now." She pointed in the direction of a mean looking boy in a suit made of green and white chewing gum. They got the impression he thought he was superior to everyone else just by the way he was standing and the way he held his head and nose high in the air.

wooosh!

Just as Bubble Gum Girl pointed to where Chewing Gum Boy was standing, he started to advance towards them, "YOU!" Chewing Gum boy growled trying but failing to be completely mean he added, "I knew you would come, you clever, sly, creative, impeccable, so and so!"

Rather than being shocked at his sister's confession, Banana-Biscuit Boy was in fits of hysterical laughter at how funny the boy's voice sounded. All of a sudden, Bubble Gum Girl shot pink **lasers** out of her large, chestnut brown eyes, "**OWWWWWWWW!** HOT!" the boy screamed like a two year old girl (no offence to two year old girls).

"Chewing Gum Boy, you stuck up, sticky, tasteless, rubbery delinquent." Banana-Biscuit Boy rolled his eyes in exasperation, "Can you two please stop your war of words?"

From out of nowhere, sticks of chewing gum came flying towards them at great speed, FWAM! FWAM! Bubble Gum Girl and Banana-Biscuit Boy were suddenly stuck to the floor, "Shut up you annoying, slippery, over ripe little banana skin!" Chewing Gum Boy yelled.

Bubble Gum Girl looked at him in surprise, "For once we actually agree on something! But when will you ever learn? The floor is *made* of sticky, green chewing gum so you don't need to fire more at us...plus it won't hold us for long. J U M P!" Bubble Gum Girl yelled.

They leapt into the humid mist that shrouded the land in **darkness** (the planet's equivalent of clouds) onto her airship. "I WANT R...E...V...E...N...G...E!" the boy shouted.

He dwelled on the REVENGE part so long that by the time he was done the siblings had already:

1) Read the revamped book 1 of this series (The Beginning),
2) Built a roller coaster and went on it multiple times,
3) Had dinner (veggie of course),
4) Lastly, rode on the roller coaster three more times,

well Banana-Biscuit Boy only once more as his salad was threatening to make a reappearance.

Finally, Chewing Gum Boy finished his 'REVENGE' but by that time, the siblings had left as they had gotten so bored. For once the villain had to move more than a few meters to find them, which he eventually did.

"Revenge? What for and why so angry?" Banana-Biscuit Boy questioned feeling confused.

Somehow, no, annoyingly, Chewing Gum Boy had jumped onto the airship, but Banana-Biscuit Boy spotted him.

"Do you like banana skins?" he asked.

"NO!" the other boy replied.

"That's a shame, 'cause you're standing on one, an especially slippery one that I created for little toads like you!"

"ARGHHHHHHHHHHHHHHHH!"

"Bye, bye!" Banana-Biscuit Boy shoved wads of sweet bubblegum into Bubble Gum Girl's mouth,

"**FIRE!**" he commanded.

His sister obeyed and shot at the sticky heap on the floor, BAM! BAM! Direct hit after direct hit she pummeled Chewing Gum Boy with soggy lumps of gum. Banana-Biscuit Boy's eyes suddenly lit up; I wonder what this **BIG RED BUTTON** does.

"Don't touch that!" yelled Bubble Gum Girl, "that triggers the…."

Banana-Biscuit Boy was promptly and directly fired into the mist, ".....ejector seat," she finished.

Once she had rescued her brother, she pushed the pink button on which was printed: **GO** - not so fast, as the person you are flying away from is really lame and slowly they began to float away.

"Wait!"

Bubble Gum Girl and Banana-Biscuit boy both turned around, "Who said that?"

Chewing Gum Boy was sprinting towards them, unfortunately (for him) he wasn't the fastest of runners so it took him a while. "I want a duel," he demanded. Both children stepped back in amazement, then hooted with laughter,

"He, he, he, ho, ho, ha!" they chuckled whilst wiping tears from their eyes.

"You challenge US to a duel?" Banana-Biscuit Boy asked incredulously, then resumed laughing.

Slowly, the Bubblegum airship drifted downwards to the sticky ground.

"So you really want a duel?" Bubble Gum Girl asked more seriously now as she saw the unchanged expression on Chewing Gum Boy's face.

"Bring it on!" Banana-Biscuit Boy yelled with kilos of confidence.

They moved into position, each in their own third. One third was made of juicy bubblegum, one third of sweet banana and biscuits and the final third of chewing gum. Bubble Gum Girl shoved a strawberry flavoured gum into her mouth and began to chew rapidly, looking much like a cement mixer. Succulent flavors flooded her tastebuds almost making her dribble just a little.

"Begin!" Chewing Gum Boy cried proudly.

Immediately, he pelted chewing gum at Bubble Gum Girl. She dodged. Banana-Biscuit Boy knew their rival would go for her first so that left him free to attack.

"Have some more banana skins!"

He aimed carefully and thrust some under his opponent's feet,

"WWWWWWAAAAAAAAAAAAAAAAAAAAAAAAA!"
the siblings battered him: Bubble Gum Girl made a forcefield
and shot pink lasers whilst her brother created wicked
swords and slashed at Chewing Gum Boy. Within minutes
their enemy realised he was being defeated.

"I surrender!" he cried.

"We're not done yet!" Banana-Biscuit Boy retorted and
turned himself into a **G I A N T** banana skin, wrapped
himself around the boy and fired him into space (not very
merciful, I know!).

They both stood gazing after him....

"He's heading towards earth!" Bubble Gum Girl exclaimed,
"we need to stop him." But then a thought crossed her
mind, "Actually, we don't need to rush, it will take him a while
to get there and I don't know about you but I'm exhausted!"

Once Bubble Gum Girl and Banana-Biscuit Boy had conquered the duel, remember, the one where they totally busted Chewing Gum Boy and sent him flying into space screaming for his mummy (possibly with wet pants too), they had felt the need to rest (all superheroes need sleep even if they have to do it in a different dimension). So they used their powers to make soft, springy beds, like not just normal springy but super, super springy. Bubble Gum Girl had to retrieve Banana-Biscuit Boy *AGAIN*, when he tried to bounce and yet again when he tried to sleep as he sank 6 METERS, almost suffocating himself. They agreed to make slightly less springy, soft beds then snuggled down under their warm duvets, completely forgetting their original purpose of stopping Chewing Gum Boy reaching earth. As soon as their heads touched their feathered pillows, they fell into a deep, deep slumber. But that night was different...they had a dream, a very vivid dream, one that told the story of when Bubble Gum Girl was little and had her memory mysteriously erased whilst happily playing and unaware of any danger. She was then delivered to earth somehow from the Bubble Gum dimension, never to see her home again. When she had awoken, she could remember nothing of her former life, only that her name was Seraphina; she had a brother called Gabriel and that she went to a school close by, oh and that she had a beloved teacher named Miss Broom, who was the best teacher ever. No one knew how and no one knew why this happened to her.

As fast as fork lightning, and at the same time, they shot out of bed with shocked and urgent expressions written across their faces.

"Who did it, who wiped the past?! " they both choroused.

They had always been able to connect in their dreams (which meant they understood each other perfectly without the need to explain) they had been able to do this since **they** were born but only when they both wanted to so a bit hit and miss really. This is a very special connection that only siblings who are really close can achieve. They didn't know anyone else that was able to do it and people seemed to think it was very strange that they could, disbelieving you might say. The news that Bubble Gum Girl had her memory wiped was a **B I G** discovery and could potentially change **e v e r y t h i n g**.

The bubble gum and banana biscuit beds disappeared as soon as the siblings leapt out of them, POOF!

"No more sleep for us then!" Banana-Biscuit Boy sighed, "we might as well head for earth!"

The two of them clambered into the airship drowsily wiping the sleep from their eyes and shaking themselves awake. As they approached the black hole again, Bubble Gum Girl looked to Gabriel with excitement and asked him,

"Okay, so Banana-Biscuit Boy, would you:

A) Like to know more facts about the balck hole, or, B)...."

"B,B,B,B,B!!!" her brother spluttered desperately.

"But I haven't even given you a second option Banana-Biscuit Boy! But if you are so sure, we'll take a tour of the black hole and I'll give you a running commentary!"

"No, have mercy on me," replied Banana-Biscuit Boy waving a little white flag frantically.

"I'll think about it..." pondered Bubble Gum Girl
(She means NO. Maybe = NO.
Errr = NO. Maybe later = NO).

But when they reached the black hole, it had nearly shrunk to the size of a pea! "Oh no!" they cried in unison. "It had been shrinking whilst we were fighting, how did we not notice!? Awwww and I really wanted to give you a tour of it!" fussed Bubble Gum Girl, disappointment etched all over her face.

"Our only hope of making it out of here is disappearing fast and you're worrying about taking a tour of it!" yelled Banana-Biscuit Boy indignantly.

Bubble Gum Girl's face scrunched up like it does when she is thinking. "Hang on, I have an idea. I can transform into bubble gum and you into a banana, right?"

"Yeah." Banana-Biscuit Boy responded.

"Then we should be small enough to squish ourselves into the shrinking black hole! We have to hurry though!" decided Bubble Gum Girl.

As fast as their powers would let them, they morphed into their fruit and sweet then launched themselves into the hole, W H O O S H ! Quickly, Bubble Gum Girl created her airship and they scrambled in.

"Phew, we're safe, what's that?" She pointed to a sticky note floating through space. Banana-Biscuit Boy grabbed it and on the front it read:

You have 3 days to prepare, then I attack..
Seriously, Chewing Gum Boy

"Errm, we may have a slight problem," he winced, "Chewing Gum Boy is going to attack us in three days!"

"WHAT!" Bubble Gum Girl screeched, she was clearly not happy about this, "that miserable, little-"

Banana-Biscuit Boy cut her off, "We need a plan."

Some moments past...

"I think we should ambush," Bubble Gum Girl declared, "it gives us the element of surprise."

"I agree," agreed her brother.

Just then a biscuit wrapper appeared and Banana-Biscuit Boy began to scribble his ideas on it:

Distract, Sneak up, ATTACK!

"Not the best plan I've ever seen," Banana-Biscuit Boy remarked about his own plan, then added: Distract (use powers), Sneak Up (use powers), Attack (use powers).

"Ah that's better, now let's go!"

Bubble Gum Girl and Banana-Biscuit Boy were trees.

"This is also not one of your best ideas," the Bubble Gum tree hissed as they waddled forward.

"It reminds me of my role in the Year 2 nativity play where I was a narrating Christmas tree! I never got the lead roles, so unfair." The siblings were in disguise trying to ambush Chewing Gum Boy at his fort on earth but so far, they were not very successful however, they were very itchy.

"I know it isn't, but it's our best shot!" her brother replied.

"Why can't we have awesome weapons and just bust in there?" she grumbled and at that exact moment, everything disappeared.

When they opened their eyes, white, fluffy clouds surrounded them and a voice boomed,

"WE MEET AGAIN BUBBLE GUM GIRL AND BANANA-BISCUIT BOY, I HAVE A LITTLE GIFT FOR YOU BOTH!"

Two amazing looking suits flew out of nowhere, one pink and blue the other orange, red and yellow.

"This…Is…Awesome!" squealed Banana-Biscuit Boy starting to squeeze himself into the pretty, pink costume.

Bubble Gum Girl snatched it out of his hands before he could get any further. "Mine little brother, not yours!"

The Supreme Ruler gave, what was supposed to be a secret chuckle, but it boomed about the place. Banana-Biscuit Boy looked a little crestfallen. Bubble Gum Girl's outfit consisted of: a skirt, top, gloves, cape and super springy boots whilst Banana-Biscuit Boy's consisted of: personalised football kit, soft, silk gloves with excellent grip, trainers and a bullet proof cape.

"NOW GO DEFEAT CHEWING GUM BOY AND SCRAP THE TREE COSTUMES, IT REALLY WASN'T WORKING!"

The supreme ruler snapped his fingers together with a smooth and satisfying CLICK! In a split second they were in Gum Boy's castle.

"Well, well, well, look who we have here!" drawled another voice.

Bubble Gum Girl gave him *the look*, she was famous for it, whenever someone annoyed her she would give them *the look* and if looks could kill, everyone who received it would be flat on their backs with their feet in the air. Hot lasers shot from her eyes,

"OWWWWW! HOT!" said the familiar sound of a two year old girl.

"Yup, that's him!" Banana-Biscuit Boy nodded knowingly.

Chewing Gum Boy slipped out from the shadows.

"Well at least I have backup!" Gum Boy announced.

And with an evil flourish, demon teachers slipped out from behind him. Those little devils had broken free. Just how they had made an escape from their clouded prisons in their last adventure, the siblings didn't know, they just knew they were on the loose.

TOP SECRET

Springy bubblegum boots

Bullet proof cape

ORIGINAL   OUTLINE   FINAL

No, No, No, No, Banana-Biscuit thought, not those demons again!!

"This won't be as easy as I thought," Bubble Gum Girl said anxiously. "What shall we do?"

"YOU have to battle ME," Chewing Gum Boy sneered slyly, but when the two superheroes saw him, they were in fits of laughter once again.

"Come on, my voice isn't that funny," he retorted.

"No, it's your pants this time!!!" When Chewing Gum Boy looked down, his saggy, slightly wet pants were **over** his suit. He looked up in alarm but refused to admit his mistake.

"Fine, we will battle you," Bubble Gum Girl said, still laughing.

"Attack!" Chewing Gum Boy bellowed.

About 10,000 demon teachers came charging at them. The children ran to the trees for cover, then Bubble Gum Girl made a force field and 10 of them bounced off the invisible wall and catapulted into outerspace. They took another 100 down with banana skins. The demons fell hard onto their backs rendering them unconscious, but suddenly the force field gave way.

"Get behind my cape," ordered Banana-Biscuit Boy.

Chewing gum continued to be pelted at them in great big, white wads, but bounced off Banana-Biscuit Boy's bulletproof cape (obviously gum proof too) rebounding onto the demons which took some of them down.

"Just another 20 to go," he uttered.

Rapidly, he loaded 20 pieces of juicy, pink bubble gum into his sister's mouth.

"Don't miss any enemies because they're the only pieces of gum we have left. FIRE!" he commanded once more.

They were now all taken down (thanks to all the practice when they fought Chewing Gum Boy previously).

"You are so busted, you are so busted!" they shouted victoriously. Just then the demons roused from their unconsciousness. Without anyone noticing, they slipped away and melted through the portcullis-like gate in defeat, until they were nothing more than distant wisps of fading broken clouds.

"No, it's not over if that's what you thought."

They both spun around in shock to see Chewing Gum Boy standing there, covered in banana slime, looking dazed but determined.

"Do you like bananas yet?" Banana-Biscuit Boy asked.

"STILL NO!" replied Chewing Gum Boy standing firm.

"Wait for it...wait for it!" Banana-Biscuit Boy chimed in again. At that precise moment, as Chewing Gum Boy stepped forward, he slipped on the ripe, blackened banana skin, sending him flying backwards. He fell so hard and fast he was sent right into space and back to where he belonged in his vast, green and white, sticky dimension where he would be keeping himself company for a long, long time hopefully. The siblings had now claimed their second victory.

The children were relaxing on their cloud sofa feeling very happy with themselves and their victory.

"We are the champions!" Banana-Biscuit Boy sang.

"My friends," Bubble Gum Girl added.

"And we'll keep on fighting, to the end," Banana-Biscuit Boy continued.

"We are the champions," Bubble Gum Girl cried, quite emotional now as she discreetly brushed away a falling tear.

"AHEM..DO YOU WANT DINNER OR WHAT?"

The Supreme Ruler interrupted with the question.

"FOOD?" Bubble Gum Girl asked

"**FOOD!**" Banana-Biscuit Boy yelled with obvious delight.

The children charged faster than kids running towards a chocolate factory handing out freebies. There in front of them was an enormous table laden with all sorts of goodies. They almost trampled the Supreme Ruler to get to it, much to his disgust.

There were: **humongous** hot-dogs, delicious desserts, **belly bulging burgers**, teeth chomping chips, sensational sweets, slurptastic soda, (just saying everything was vegetarian) a bowl of flourishing fruit and especially for the children... piles of **bubblegum, banana and biscuits**. Famished, they delved into the edible treasures and scoffed to their hearts' delight.

"I'd like to see how Chewing Gum Boy is fairing now, probably scavenging around to find some morsels to eat...maybe scavenging in dustbins whilst we're here..." wondered Seraphina to herself but out loud, not quite finishing her sentence. Banana-Biscuit Boy finished for her, "ftuffing our fafes," he chuckled as bits of banana and goodness knows what else sprayed from his mouth as he spluttered his "S"s and "F"s.

"Perhaps we should just concentrate on eating rather than speaking," suggested his sister as she picked bits of mashed up food out of her hair.

So as fast as they could, they ate every single last bit of food. "Brother, where are you?" Bubble Gum Girl said as she couldn't see him over her humongous stomach. Luckily, her outfit was elasticated.

"I'm over here!" replied Banana-Biscuit Boy.

"We might suffer after eating that much food. Not sure it was the best thing to do...eat everything in sight I mean!" Bubble Gum Girl reflected.

THE END (We Promise)

"Ahhhhh!" The children leaned back, they were exhausted, all they wanted to do now was sit back and relax! However, the Supreme Ruler had other ideas and made them run five laps of his mansion, (by the way his mansion is the size of Luxembourg),

"MUST KEEP YOU TWO IN GOOD SHAPE!" he kept chanting as they passed him on every lap.

"But round **IS** a shape!" the children piped in.

Once they were done and got their breathing under control, Banana-Biscuit Boy looked lost in thought one moment then suddenly announced, "I wish I could bounce high like you." He pondered over the fact that his powers were all about bananas and biscuits, not bubble gum.

"What makes you wish that?" Bubble Gum Girl asked as she looked at him **questioningly**.

"I just think it's so *cool* to jump the way you do," he said.

With a dramatic pause, the *Supreme Ruler* boomed,

"WELL...WHY NOT TAKE A LOOK IN YOUR GARDEN!" With a flourish of his hands, he pointed in the direction of their home. Bubble Gum Girl and Banana-Biscuit Boy raced to the edge of the fluffy, white clouds wondering what this had to do with anything.

Far off in the distance they spied something. They could see it was rounded in shape and looked new with a black patch in the middle, but couldn't quite work out what it was. In anticipation, the siblings squealed with delight, "Bye Bye! Thanks for everything," they chorused.

The children crossed their arms over their chests and leaned back confidently off the edge of the cloud. SPROING!

Yet again, they landed on a bubble that sank and enveloped them before bouncing them back to the Supreme Ruler.

"Ooopsie, we'll be gone in a jiffy!" Bubble Gum Girl apologised.

The children lived in a small, *humble* house on a small estate and in their back garden, awarded to them was a ...... T R A M P O L I N E! It was the biggest, springiest, most amazing **trampoline** they had ever seen.

"Wahey, this is better than *cloud* jumping," yelled Banana-Biscuit Boy as he did a backward triple somersault landing perfectly steady on his feet. And it was in that moment, he realised that you don't always need superpowers to have fun!

We now have to say goodbye to Seraphina (Bubble Gum Girl) and Gabriel (Banana-Biscuit Boy) and leave them to enjoy their supreme gift. We have come to the end of this adventure, again, however, we may still see more of these heroes in another adventure, Book 3, who knows!

The End
(This is the last time... for now, promise)

THANKS TO:

Uncle Lee O'Brien
for all the graphics in our books
(we know we were very demanding so sent you Gin as a thanks)
and encouraging us to write.
We love you.

Rachael Taylor
for always believing in us and supporting us in and out of school.

All
those who bought book 1 and helped raise money for
the NHS and an extra special thanks to those who
wrote wonderful reviews.
Without your feedback and support we wouldn't
have continued writing.

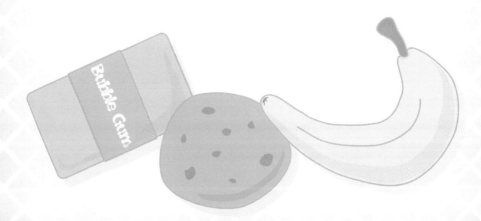

S&G
Productions

ISBN: 9798587202566

Printed in Great Britain
by Amazon